WELCOME TO
PASSPORT TO READING
A beginning reader's ticket to a brand-new world!

Every book in this program is designed to build read-along and read-alone skills, level by level, through engaging and enriching stories. As the reader turns each page, he or she will become more confident with new vocabulary, sight words, and comprehension.

These PASSPORT TO READING levels will help you choose the perfect book for every reader.

READING TOGETHER
Read short words in simple sentence structures together to begin a reader's journey.

READING OUT LOUD
Encourage developing readers to sound out words in more complex stories with simple vocabulary.

READING INDEPENDENTLY
Newly independent readers gain confidence reading more complex sentences with higher word counts.

READY TO READ MORE
Readers prepare for chapter books with fewer illustrations and longer paragraphs.

This book features sight words from the educator-supported Dolch Sight Words List. This encourages the reader to recognize commonly used vocabulary words, increasing reading speed and fluency.

For more information, please visit passporttoreadingbooks.com.

Enjoy the journey!

Little, Brown and Company

Hachette Book Group
1290 Avenue of the Americas, New York, NY 10104
Visit us at lb-kids.com

Little, Brown and Company is a division of Hachette Book Group, Inc.
The Little, Brown name and logo are trademarks of Hachette Book Group, Inc.

The publisher is not responsible for websites (or their content) that are not owned by the publisher.

First Edition: June 2015

ISBN 978-0-316-37853-6

10 9 8 7 6 5 4 3 2 1

CW

Printed in the United States of America

Passport to Reading titles are leveled by independent reviewers applying the standards developed by Irene Fountas and Gay Su Pinnell in *Matching Books to Readers: Using Leveled Books in Guided Reading*, Heinemann, 1999.

Meet Rosetta

By Celeste Sisler

LITTLE, BROWN AND COMPANY
New York • Boston

Attention, Disney Fairies fans!
Look for these words when you read
this book. Can you spot them all?

flowers

dress

feather

garden

Rosetta is a garden-talent fairy.

She likes to grow flowers.

Rosetta plays dress-up in her room.

Her red-and-pink

dress is so pretty.

Next, she dresses up
as a pirate fairy!
Her hat has

a big white feather.

After dressing up,

Rosetta wants to

have a garden party.

Tinker Bell comes over
to help get ready.
The two friends
clean up Rosetta's room.

Tinker Bell and Rosetta
put on their dresses.

The other fairies come over.

They all look so pretty!

After the fairies
eat and drink,
they go outside
to the garden.

In the garden,
they laugh,
dance, and sing.

At night, the
fairies fly back
to their rooms.

They are sleepy

after a fun night.

The next day, the fairies get
together and thank Rosetta.
They tell Rosetta
she is special, too.

Rosetta smiles.
She loves her friends
and being a garden-
talent fairy.